W9-CCN-014

MAKING
FRIENDS

First edition for the United States, Canada,
and the Philippines published 1991
by Barron's Educational Series, Inc.

Design David West Children's Book Design

© Copyright by Aladdin Books, Ltd 1991

All rights reserved.
No part of this book may be reproduced in any form
by photostat, microfilm, xerography, or any other
means, or incorporated into any information retrieval
system, electronic or mechanical, without the written
permission of the copyright owner.

All inquiries should be addressed to:
Barron's Educational Series, Inc.
250 Wireless Boulevard
Hauppauge, NY 11788

International Standard Book No. 0-8120-4660-9

Library of Congress Catalog Card No. 91-14193

Library of Congress Cataloging-in Publication Data

Petty, Kate.
Making Friends / Kate Petty. -- 1st ed.
p. cm. -- (Playgrounds)
Summary: Jack does not understand that friendship must be a two-way street until he meets Richard.
ISBN 0-8120-4660-9
[1. Friendship--Fiction.] I. Title. II. Series: Petty, Kate.
Playgrounds.
PZ7.P44814Mak 1991
[E]--dc20 91-14193 CIP AC

Printed in Belgium
4 98765

Kate Petty and Charlotte Firmin

Barron's

Jack's sister, Jane, has lots of friends.
Even when they're not playing together,
they talk to each other on the phone.
It drives Jack's mom crazy.

Jack would love to have a good friend.

He really tries to make friends.

But something always goes wrong.

"I don't know why," says Jack.

"I think I'm a friendly person."

On the way to school Jane and Jack
meet Jane's friend, Rosie.
Rosie's brother, Richard, is there, too.
Jack likes Richard.

When they arrive at school some other children gather around the two boys.

"Four eyes," they tease Richard.

Jack laughs at Richard, too.

"Four eyes – that's a funny name."

Rosie comes over to comfort Richard.
Jane comes, too. She is furious with Jack.

"You should have stood up for Richard.
I always stand up for my friends," she says.

Jack is sorry.
"Richard will never want
to be my friend now," he thinks.
"But I'll try to make up with him."

Jack hangs his coat next to Richard's.
He starts to tell Richard all about
a cartoon he saw the other night.
He goes through the whole long plot
and does all the voices.

Richard wants to tell Jack that he saw the cartoon ages ago, but he can't. Jack chatters on and on and it's hard to stop him. Richard goes off to find someone else to talk to.

"What did I do wrong?" he asks Toby.

"You were just being boring."

"No I wasn't. I was being interesting!"

"Maybe *you* thought so," says Toby,
"But you were so busy talking that
you wouldn't listen to Richard.
Nobody will listen to you for long
if you won't listen to them too."

Jane can see that Jack is unhappy. "I'm going to play at Rosie's house this weekend. Do you want to come and play with Richard?" she asks.

"He thinks I'm boring and that
I don't stick up for him,"
Jack mumbles.

But he soon cheers up.
"I will come," he says. "I can take
some snacks and share them with him.
That might make him like me."

Richard really enjoys the snacks.
The boys are watching TV but Jack wants to play outside. He switches off the TV.
"Hey, I was watching that."

"TV's boring. Come and play outside," says Jack.

"No," shouts Richard. "I don't want to play outside. But you can go. I don't want to play with you anymore, anyway."

Miss Wade sees Jack sitting by himself
in class. When she asks him how he is
he tells her all about the weekend.
"You must learn to work things out
with your friends, Jack," she says.

"It's silly to lose a friend just because you want to do different things. Why not find something else to do together that you both enjoy?"

"I didn't think Richard was my friend,
anyway," says Jack sadly.
"I think you'll find that he is,"
says Miss Wade.
"Come on, Jack," calls Richard.
"Let's build a castle."

Actually, Jack wants to draw instead.
But he thinks for a minute before saying,
"You build a castle. I'll draw it."
"Terrific!" thinks Miss Wade,
and gives a sigh of relief.

Builder and artist ... Richard and Jack make a good team, don't they?

THINGS TO DO...

Draw a picture of Jack and Richard or Jane and Rosie.
Or draw a picture of your friend.

Talk about what Jack wants.
Or talk about what happens when Jack goes to Richard's house.

Make up a play or use puppets to show how two people can stay friends even though one wants to play a computer game and the other one wants to play with Legos.

Remember that it's not always easy to be a friend. Here are some things that make people friends:

They stick up for each other.
They take turns to listen to each other.
They share.
They sometimes let the other one have their own way.

Can you think of any more?